S

D0211234

Dear Parents:

Congratulations! Your child is taking the first steps on an exciting journey. The destination? Independent reading!

STEP INTO READING® will help your child get there. The program offers five steps to reading success. Each step includes fun stories and colorful art or photographs. In addition to original fiction and books with favorite characters, there are Step into Reading Non-Fiction Readers, Phonics Readers and Boxed Sets, Sticker Readers, and Comic Readers—a complete literacy program with something to interest every child.

Learning to Read, Step by Step!

Ready to Read   Preschool–Kindergarten
• big type and easy words • rhyme and rhythm • picture clues
For children who know the alphabet and are eager to begin reading.

Reading with Help   Preschool–Grade 1
• basic vocabulary • short sentences • simple stories
For children who recognize familiar words and sound out new words with help.

Reading on Your Own   Grades 1–3
• engaging characters • easy-to-follow plots • popular topics
For children who are ready to read on their own.

Reading Paragraphs   Grades 2–3
• challenging vocabulary • short paragraphs • exciting stories
For newly independent readers who read simple sentences with confidence.

Ready for Chapters   Grades 2–4
• chapters • longer paragraphs • full-color art
For children who want to take the plunge into chapter books but still like colorful pictures.

STEP INTO READING® is designed to give every child a successful reading experience. The grade levels are only guides; children will progress through the steps at their own speed, developing confidence in their reading.

Remember, a lifetime love of reading starts with a single step!

created by

Stephen Hillenburg

Visit us on the Web!
StepIntoReading.com
rhcbooks.com

Educators and librarians, for a variety of teaching tools, visit us at RHTeachersLibrarians.com

ISBN 978-0-593-37402-3 (trade) — ISBN 978-0-593-37403-0 (lib. bdg.)

Printed in the United States of America

10 9 8 7 6 5 4 3 2 1

KAMP KORAL
SPONGEBOB'S UNDER YEARS

SNACK ATTACK!

by Elle Stephens

based on the teleplay "Midnight Snack Attack" by Luke Brookshier

illustrated by Dave Aikins

Random House 🏠 New York

It is breakfast time
at Kamp Koral.
SpongeBob and Patrick
wait in line.
They are hungry!

Patrick gets eggs that jump.

SpongeBob's bread is too hard.

Squidward's cereal is alive.

Sandy's pancakes are terrible.

The food here stinks!

After breakfast,
a counselor tells the campers
to go to Lake Yuckymuck.
It is Slap Line Fun Time!

"Yay!" cheer the campers.

They love Slap Line Fun Time.

The campers leave.
Plankton cleans up
the kitchen.

Then he goes
to his secret lab.
"Hello, Mr. Plankton,"
says Karen,
his computer assistant.

SNACKS

Plankton is working
on a secret project.
It is a mind-bending
vending machine!
He calls it
the Bender Vendor.

1 2 3
4 5 6
7 8 9
A B C
D E F

RETURN

PUSH

It is filled with mutant snacks!
Anyone who eats them
will turn into a mutant.
Plankton will use the mutants
to take over the world!

At the lake,
SpongeBob and Patrick
play Slap Line Fun Time.
Sandy plays, too!

"Watch out, y'all!"
yells Sandy.
"Nice one, Sandy!"
says SpongeBob.

Soon it is dinnertime.
SpongeBob and Patrick
want to keep playing.
They sneak off
the dinner line.

They play on the Slap Line

for hours and hours.

Then SpongeBob gets hungry.

Oh, no!
The kitchen is closed.
"We missed dinner!"
says SpongeBob.

Patrick has an idea.

"Let's sneak in

and grab some food,"

he says.

He opens the window.

The friends do not find
any food.
But they do find
Plankton's secret lab!

They see the mind-bending
vending machine.
"That looks like food
we can actually eat!"
says Patrick.

Karen helps them
get some snacks out.
She forgets to tell them
they are mutant snacks.

SpongeBob and Patrick
eat all the snacks.
They turn into mutants!

When Plankton finds out,
he is afraid he will get fired.
He has to find a way
to change SpongeBob
and Patrick back.
He gets to work.

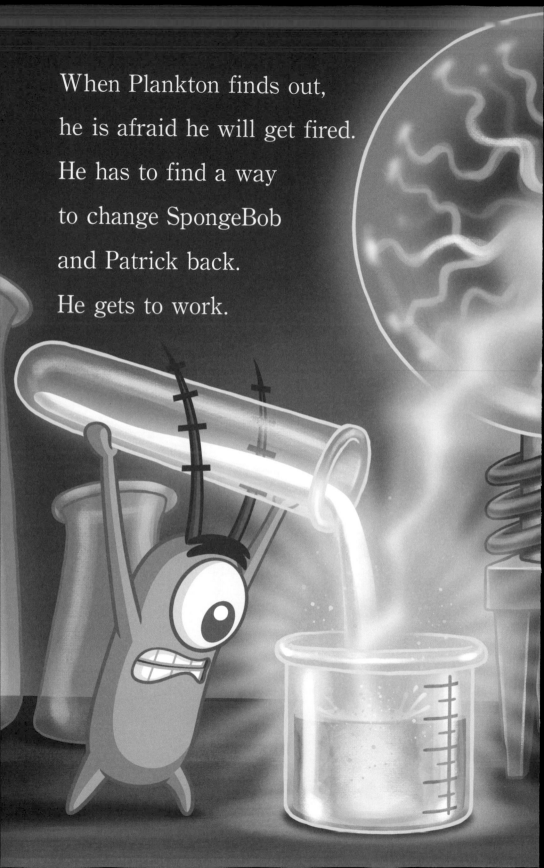

"Yes!" he cries
when he creates
the right formula.
Now he has to find
SpongeBob and Patrick.

The mutant friends
are busy having fun.
They scare
the other campers.

They have
super-fast races!

SpongeBob and Patrick
go back to the Slap Line.
"Ooh-wee! What happened
to you?" asks Sandy.

"We're trying out our new look,"
says Patrick.
They ride the Slap Line
straight into Sandy.

Sandy goes flying—
right into Plankton!
He still cannot find
SpongeBob and Patrick.

Just then—*snap!*
SpongeBob and Patrick
break the Slap Line!
They fall into the lake.

Plankton spots
the mutant friends
on the shore.

He injects them
with his formula!
It hits them!

SpongeBob and Patrick
return to regular size.
"Aww," says Patrick. "Being
a mutant was so much fun!"